W9-DGE-940

Splish, Splash!

story by Sarah Weeks
pictures by Ashley Wolff

To Pat Martinez,
with love and admiration
—S. W.

For Rory
—A. W.

HarperCollins®, ☰®, and I Can Read Book®
are trademarks of HarperCollins Publishers Inc.

Splish, Splash!
Text copyright © 1999 by Sarah Weeks
Illustrations copyright © 1999 by Ashley Wolff
Printed in the U.S.A. All rights reserved.

Library of Congress Cataloging-in-Publication Data
Weeks, Sarah.
  Splish, splash! / story by Sarah Weeks ; pictures by Ashley Wolff.
    p.   cm. — (My first I can read book)
Summary: Different animals ask to join a fish in a tub until the tub is full.
  ISBN 0-06-027892-7. — ISBN 0-06-027893-5 (lib. bdg.)
  ISBN 0-06-444282-9 (pbk.)
  [1. Animals—Fiction.   2. Stories in rhyme.]   I. Wolff, Ashley, ill.
II. Title.   III. Series.
PZ8.3.W4125Sp   1999   98-20028
[E]—dc21   CIP
                                           AC

First Harper Trophy edition, 2000

Visit us on the World Wide Web!
www.harperchildrens.com

Splish, Splash!

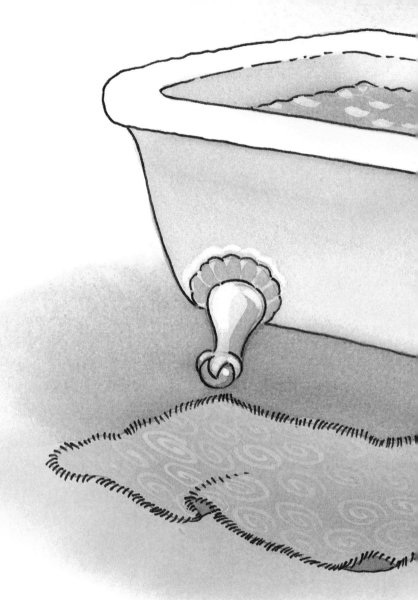

This is Chub.

This is his tub.

He loves to sit in it and scrub.

"Make room for me!"

6

"Can you fit three?"

"Jump in if you wish!"

says Chub the fish.

And they splish
and they splash,

and they splash
and they splish.

"Am I too tall?"

10

"Am I too small?"

"Am I too big?"

"No, not at all!

Jump in if you wish!"

says Chub the fish.

And they splish
and they splash,

and they splash
and they splish.

"Am I too short?"

"Am I too thin?"

"Am I too fat?"

"May I come in?"

"Jump in if you wish!"

says Chub the fish.

19

And they splish
and they splash,

and they splash
and they splish.

"This tub is full,"
says the bull.
"And that is that,"
says the cat.

"No more will fit,"
says the rat.
"That's it."

"No room for me?"

says the bug.

"Not a bit!"

"Too bad," says the bug.

"I'm sad."

"Make room for the bug
or I'll pull out the plug!
Make room," says Chub,
"and don't make a fuss.

There's room in the tub
for all of us."

The bull says,

"Bug, jump in if you wish."

The cat says,

"You will fit if we squish."

"Hooray for Chub!
Hooray for the tub!"

"Hooray for us all,"
says Chub the fish.

And they splish
and they splash,
and they splash
and they splish.